Rowan

THROUGH THE VEIL

Rowan

Through the veil

Sheesha Shapiro

DEDICATION

To my hippie mom if it wasn't for you I wouldn't have had the courage to embrace the world and all the sensations in it. You're my universe if I didn't see you through the week, I'll see you through the window.

I want you alone with me.

Just to hold your naked body on top of mine,

To see where they fit

Waiting for them to fall into place, almost by themselves.

To feel as though our souls need to cry with utter joy.

Race on heart

Be the first one to catch me.

Run on with Godspeed

Only to find that I've been here waiting,

For a simple tap on the shoulder,

To be presented with such exquisite beauty,

Only to have my own heart begin to race

And run circles

'Round yours.

~ Chapter 1 ~

The alarm went off on the clock radio and the song "White Wedding" by Billy Idol filled her bedroom. Half awake, Rowan fumbled for the snooze button one last time.

It was the last day of senior year and Rowan couldn't help shake that familiar feeling. A feeling that had been there since childhood and in the last few weeks it was becoming stronger. The feeling of being watched.

"You're going to be late!" her mother yelled from downstairs of their two storied craftsman house.

"I'll be right down," Rowan mumbled through a yawn.

Throwing back the patchwork quilt her grandmother had made for her 12th birthday, Rowan sat there trying to remember the night's dream but the harder she tried the farther away it became.

Grabbing a black mini skirt, the Madonna t-shirt she got from her last concert and the black and white high-top converse from her closet she again had a nagging feeling that someone or something was watching her. Turning toward her open bedroom door the feeling dissipated and all she could see was the rug her mother made from different colored carpet squares, that as a child she would use as a hopscotch board.

Rowen shuffled her feet down the hallway. The scent of fried bacon and eggs hovered making her stomach churn. Lately the site of anything that came from an animal made her sick.

Since she had showered before bed getting ready would be quick.

The one and only bathroom in the house was small. Perhaps even too small. There was a clawfoot tub her mother painted into a pink pig with eyelashes and lipstick, a toilet to the right and a small sink to the left. The door had to be removed years ago due to lack of space and was replaced with a red paisley curtain.

The water felt great as she splashed it on her face. Rowan never thought much about her appearance. Her dark lashes were long which only made her green eyes appear more vibrant against her fair skin. Her mother once said she had cupid lips because her bottom lip was so full and a deep pink. Looking into the mirror Rowan ran her fingers through her long wavy auburn hair and tried to imagine what her best friend Anna had up her sleeve.

"It's our last day of school Roe...trust me," Anna said before hanging up the phone the night before. Anna was one of the few people Rowan could trust, actually she and Tonya were the only girls she had ever trusted besides her mother.

Entering the pink kitchen Rowan could see her mom at the other end trying to attach a pink and orange beaded curtain in the door frame that separated the kitchen and her art room. If Rowan was to describe her in one word it would be "grace."

Grabbing an apple from the white bowl in the center of the table and taking a bite, Rowan kissed her mom and then blew a kiss to the poster of David Coverdale that was hung on the basement door and proceeded out the front and into the warm Miami Beach heat.

****

"What took you so long?" Anna asked as Rowan jumped into the black Nissan 300zx. Anna's new ride was a birthday present from her dominant Cuban father and docile mother. They reminded her of Fred and Wilma Flinstone but with a mafia edge. There was such a big difference between their two worlds. Rowan's single mom was a hippy from the 60's that gave up her career as a ballerina to raise her on a very modest income. Shit, they didn't even own a car until this year and Anna came from money. Her family ran several businesses and lived in a gated community on the bay. Their house was pristine but sterile and lacked the comfort and color Rowans home oozed.

"Sorry about that. I hit snooze too many times," Rowan shouted over the obnoxious sound of the Bangles blaring from the stereo.

Pulling into the school parking lot Rowan could see the pastel cliché in the far left quad. Anna dubbed them that because they always wore pastel colored overalls with bright matching bows in their hair. If you listened to their sweet valley-girl personalities too long one would get a toothache. To the right the dead heads gathered around a palm tree passing a feather adorned roach clip while one strummed Led Zeppelin on her guitar.

"Did you tell her? Did you tell her?" squealed Tonya as she skipped towards them, swaying her long blonde ponytail from side to side and flashing her newly straightened teeth.

Tonya was wearing a long white skirt that folded below her belly button, a hot pink crop top with the same color gelee slides.

"No..and I don't plan on it," Anna sang back.

"Ugh...why not? I'm just bursting at the seams!!!" Tonya whined while applying another coat of lip potion lip gloss.

Anna and Tonya continued to head toward the entrance of the school while bantering the pros and cons of revealing the big surprise. Rowan bent down to tie her sneaker when that all too familiar sensation crept up the back of her neck, making the hair on her arms stand on end. "Not now" she whispered to herself. Then, out of the corner of her eye, something or someone moved behind one of the buttonwood trees that lined the perimeter of the student parking lot. Standing up and facing in the direction of the movement and seeing nothing, Rowan chalked it up to "her overactive imagination" and sprinted to class.

The third bell rang and everyone quickly headed towards their last day of childhood.

~ You are charmingly delicious ~

~Chapter 2~

It was dark and Rowan was descending a staircase she didn't recognize.

It wasn't the staircase that climbed to the left of her living room. This staircase was made of limestone and it felt damp on her bare feet. Her white full cotton slip clung to her figure.

The banging on the large birch door became louder, firmer. Whomever was on the other side was determined to be answered.

Continuing toward the sound a fog rolled in from underneath the door, circling Rowan's feet, like a snake twisting around its prey. The fogs smooth texture on her bare skin sent a shiver up her thighs and a warmth in her cheeks.

"Why aren't you ready?" Anna questioned as she shook Rowan awake.

"I must have dozed off," Rowan groaned as she rubbed the dream from her eyes.

Sitting on the edge of her double bed Tonya began popping her gum and teasing out her hair. Rowan swore Tonya was the queen of Aqua net.

"Well wake up and get dressed in the most head banging outfit you've got... and make it sexy!"

"Is this sexy enough for my surprise?" Rowan asked as she stepped out from behind her oriental dressing screen.

Rowan turned slowly so Anna and Tonya could take it all in. She had seen a model wear something like what she had thrown together on MTV and from the smiles on her friend's faces it was a hit.

Rowan's mom was out for the night teaching a painting class at the local civic center so she didn't have to worry about being told to dress her age. "Hang on to your childhood," she would constantly say when Rowan wore her eyeliner too thick or bared too much skin. But tonight, without a parental eye, Rowan applied her makeup dark, emphasizing her almond shaped eyes and full lips. Her black leather shorts hugged her curves, barely covering her ass, as her fishnet stocking formed perfectly to her long legs. Her black tank top stretched Pat Benetar's face nicely across her chest. Slipping on her black pumps and a stack of black rubber bracelets, the three girls piled into Anna's car and sped towards Ocean Drive. Blaring Bon Jovi on the radio.

Pulling into a parking lot along the beach the three girls stepped out of the air- conditioned car and into the humid ocean breeze.
"Surprise!" Both girls sang while throwing their arms up in the air. Rowan could hear the bass vibrate from the tall gray building in front of them.
The streetlamps no longer worked which gave the neon sign "The Kitchen Club" an eerie glow. If one walked by it in the daytime you'd think it was just another run down hotel. Ocean and Collins Drive was lined with them. Revitalization had just begun but this part of town

was still littered with hookers and transients and all the pastel colors from the 1950's had faded away creating a ghost town.

Rowan was hesitant but excited all at once. They had always talked about going but that was it, it was just talk. And now here they were. Only the coolest of people cruised the halls of the Kitchen Club and they were about to step into the oven.

As the girls were handing over their IDs to the doorman, who looked as though his main job was running a motorcycle gang, Rowan's attention was drawn towards the guy stamping other patrons' hands just a few feet away with the words "heaven vs. hell" in neon for everyone entering.
He was tall with long black hair and dark eyes and when he looked in her direction Rowan swore there was a hint of violet in them. He was hot and Rowan found herself wondering what it would be like to kiss him.
It was her turn to have her hand stamped, and as he let his hand linger on her wrist, for what seemed to be forever, she felt as though they had met before. Which was impossible, he certainly wasn't from her school and from the way he looked, he had to be at least 5 years older than her.
"Welcome to the Kitchen Club," he said as Rowan pulled back her hand. "I'm Amias." "Well that's an interesting name. How do you pronounce it?" Rowan shouted over the loud music.
"Ah-mee-us," he shouted back as Anna pulled her away from his intense gaze. Rowan took one last glance over her shoulder offering a

quick smile and mouthed "Come dance with us," before being pulled into the main foyer.

The layout of the Kitchen Club hadn't changed from when it was a hoping hotel in the 1950's. But the colors were no longer ocean hues. The entire place was painted black. The paintings on the walls glowed in the black lighting. To the left of the grand foyer was a room with a bar that ran the entire length of the hotel. It was buzzing with fellow clubbers waiting on their drinks as the smoke from their cigarettes billowed above. The tables were stained a dark mahogany, the legs carved into imps with outstretched arms holding its marble top. The oversized high back chairs were all carved as well and upholstered in a velvet of deep purple.

Ahead of them was a stage that sat five feet above the dance floor adorn in the same velvet with two huge gargoyles on each end. She could see a band setting up for later as the crowd danced below to some heavy metal song.

To her right was another room lined with the same chairs but its back wall was completely glass that opened up onto a marble patio with an in ground pool in its center. To the right of the pool Rowan could see steps that took you right down onto the beach.

"Anna, this place is awesome."

"We did well?"

"You did better than good." The music had changed to something familiar.

"You ready to shake this place up?"

"When am I not?"

"Then let's go. The dance floor is waiting and we need to pour some of that sugar."

Holding each other's hands, the girls moved through the maze of bodies until they reached the dance floor.

The fog machine and black lighting darkened the room making it hard for Rowan to see beyond her friends. Continuing to move to the beat of the music she tried to picture what it would be like to dance with Amias. And what was up with those violet eyes?

Rowan, caught up in her own thoughts, didn't notice that she had a visitor until it was too late. She could feel the warmth of the stranger's chest pressed against her back and the firmness of his right hand as it moved across her bare stomach. Instead of being startled and turning around, Rowan felt at ease, almost hypnotized by the slow and calming tingling she was absorbing from her unknown dance partner.

"I'm so glad you decided to join me," Rowan shouted over the music as she continued to grind against him. She had never been this brazen before but with both friends giving her a two thumbs-up, why not. Rowan reached above with her left arm and placed her hand behind the stranger's neck twisting her fingers into his hair and with her right hand she moved his to her thigh. She could feel his hardness against her and the softness of his lips as he licked at her ear.

When the song faded into Billy Idol's "White Wedding," Rowan turned around to thank Amias for joining her only to be startled to find it wasn't Amias she was dirty dancing with. Standing before her was a man with features so striking she had to catch her breath. He stood around 6'2, with skin as fair as hers. His strawberry blonde hair was disheveled from Rowan's fingers and it laid just below his collar bone. He was wearing tight leather pants, a black wife beater with the words "The Clash" across it, and around his neck was a brown leather strap that held a Celtic emblem. What made him so striking to Rowan was his green eyes? These were not just any pair of green eyes but the brightest green with flakes of gold. The same color as hers.

"They're playing our song," he said while undressing her with those eyes.

"Is that so?" Rowan questioned as she attempted to gain her composure. Embarrassment for being so unadulterated with this stranger.

"I'm sorry but I don't normally dance that way and if I led you on I didn't mean to." Rowan attempted to escape his eyes and the feeling that if she surrendered to this desire she would never find her way back.

"There you are!!!" Anna said as she and Tonya approached the two of them.

"Hey sexy... we're going to steal our girl now." Anna grabbed Rowan's hand leading her to the barroom.

Tonya found an empty table in the corner. Each one had a burning candle that emitted a golden glow through the darkness. Handing her and Anna a "Sex on the Beach" cocktail Tonya plopped her herself down grinning from ear to ear.

"So? Who was the Viking you were dirty dancing with? She asked while attempting to tie her cherry stem with her tongue.

"Yes, do tell," questioned Anna.

Stirring her drink with her black polished finger Rowan shrugged her shoulders.   But somewhere in the back of her mind, she had a feeling she did.

      The banging got louder but this time instead of being in her living room Rowan was standing in a cave. Her feet softly sinking into the moss-covered floor as she walked further into it.

Hanging from the walls were lit torches illuminating a massive mural of what looked to be a battle of some sort. The sight of the dead surrounded by a tall figure made her furror her brow. Well this isn't a good sign she heard herself saying. Cautiously, she continuing to walk in the direction of the noise but by the time she reached the end of the hall the banging had stopped. She could hear someone whispering in her head. It was a male voice, "I've waited so long for you." The latch on the door creaked as she opened.

Standing there was Amias. His face was far from friendly. His eyes were stern, his cheeks red with anger. Rowan could feel a scream rise up from her core, only to hear silence. Unable to look away, she watched him mouth "I will find you" before evaporating to the sound of her clock radio going off suggesting she should "Walk like an Egyptian."

~ I will forever see your face and feel your presence,

I will always love you………….. As I always have,

But now with an emotion and bond that will be tied

With silver chain ~

~ Chapter 3 ~

It had been three weeks since the girl's night out and Rowan was having a hard time focusing on her birthday.

She would be turning 19 on the eve of the summer solstice and Anna thought a beach bonfire would be the perfect setting. In all honesty, she just wanted to stay home. She didn't feel it was all that special and lately the feeling of being watched was becoming a distraction. At night when her mom was off teaching a class or working late at St. Christopher's rectory filing papers for the new priest, she found herself reluctant to leave the safety of her home.

Still lying in the coziness of her bed Rowan's mom fluttered in carrying her favorite carrot and zucchini muffin, topped with a candle and singing her rendition of Happy Birthday.

"How's my little bluebird picked in the summertime?"

Rowan sat up and hugged her mom. The scent of her lavender perfume made her feel calm and safe.

"I thought you'd like to wear what I got you to your bonfire tonight," holding up two boxes, both wrapped in Garfield wrapping paper.

"Really mom? Garfield?"

"What? I thought it was funny. You used to love Garfield."

"The key word is "use to" and I was like 8."

Roan unwrapped the larger box first, finding a black slip dress inside. The smaller box held a leather choker with a Celtic medallion in the center. The same medallion her mysterious dance partner had worn. "I love it! But where did you find this? Holding the choker in her hands.

"I've been keeping it for years just waiting for the right time to give it to you." Brushing the hair from her daughter's eyes Isleen knew what she was about to tell her was going to open up a part of her life she would prefer to keep locked away.

"It was your fathers."

"Excuse me? My what?"

"Your fathers."

Rowan's mind started spinning with so many questions. Her mother never spoke about her father. All she ever told her was that they had met on a September night during the annual Fairy festival. They had a brief romance and then he disappeared.

And now, in the palm of her hand was a connection and an emptiness that began to open a hole into her heart.

****

Anna insisted that Rowan meet her and the rest of the party at the beach behind the Kitchen Club. She said it wouldn't be perfect unless Rowan made a grand entrance into adulthood.

Wearing her hair in a messy bun, the black slip dress and choker her mother gave her earlier, Rowan slipped into a taxi that would take her back to the place her body got its first taste of fire.

The sun was setting in an orange and pink sky when the taxi pulled up. The air was warm and she could taste the salt on her lips. When she reached the end of the wooden bridge that carried her from the parking lot to the beach, Rowen bent down, took off her doc martens and headed towards the music.

"You were supposed to make a grand entrance!!" Anna said while doing a body shot off Tonya.
"Sorry to disappoint," Rowan replied with a side smile and a wink at Tonya as she licked the leftover salt off her chest.
Around the bonfire were several of their friends from school. A few had graduated the year before and it was nice to see them sitting on the lounge chairs drinking OV splits while the "Pretenders" played on a boom box.
It felt good. Tonight her guard was down and Rowan was exactly where she wanted to be.

A bit tipsy and worn out from playing frisbee in the dark Rowan sat back into one of the chairs and buried her toes into the cool sand. She laughed to herself as Tonya attempted to run in her neon green mini skirt, failing miserably.
"I hear it's your birthday," Amias said, taking the seat next to her.
"Mhmm, yes it is. So what are you gifting me?"
Amias broke into a low chuckle. Rubbing both his hands up and down his ripped jeans he leaned over and whispered, "You have no idea. Come with me."
Amias offered his hand and without hesitation Rowen took it.

Before they got a few feet away Anna yelled asking where she was going, told her to have fun and headed into the Kitchen Club.

Amias continued to hold Rowan's hand as he walked her along the shoreline towards a large line of rocks that jutted out, bracing the waves as they crashed. He was trying to stay focused on his intent but the softness of her skin and the scent of her patchouli perfume began to distract him. A form of distraction that wasn't allowed.

As they neared the cliff of rocks Rowan stopped, planting herself firmly in the sand.

"If you plan on climbing those rocks... I'm out. And if you think I'm going to climb those rocks...I'm double out."

He knew this wasn't going to be easy but time was of the essence.

God he wanted to lay his lips upon hers and catch her flighty tongue between his teeth.

What the hell was she doing to him?

"We are not climbing, we are going inside."

"Oh? And how do you suppose we do that? Are you a magician now?

"Not exactly. Watch."

Amias placed several colored stones in front of the rocks.

Rowan watched in awe as a door slowly took shape. Rowan's recent dreams started flashing before her eyes. This has to be a trick of the moon and the three vodka and lemonades. A door doesn't just appear out of nowhere.

But in fact, it was real. And like her dreams... she was opening the door.

Amias led her across the threshold and into the cave.

There were no torches on the walls to light their way. Instead the moss-covered floor and the quartz crystals that jutted from the ceiling, glowed a bright green and violet.

"I don't understand. How is this possible?"

Rowan's head began to spin with questions.

Seeing the uneasiness in her eyes Amias wrapped his arms around her, gently kissing the top of her head. Lifting her chin, Amias looked into the eyes that have caused his longing for so long.

"You have been my life's mission for centuries." Amias brought his lips to hers, their tongues fluttered and he could feel his blood become stronger, healthier.

All Rowan wanted to do was feed him kisses. Her nails traced the fine features of his face as he lifted her, wrapping her bare legs around his waist. The sensation of a thousand sparks turned into a throbbing. Rowan began to grind against his chest.

Amias abandoned all restraint and moaned. He too felt those fiery sparks. Reaching under her dress he grabbed her ass pulled her even closer.

"Take me." Rowan leaned back so his kisses could fall onto her shoulders, her neck. What little Rowan was wearing became too much, she wanted to be set free.

His hands slipped under her panties to find her wetness delightful. He hungered to lap up the juices that made it so easy for his fingers to move in and out.

Stepping back to see her pleasure, Amias's eyes fell upon the Celtic choker.

"Where did you get that?"

Noticing that his demeanor had changed Rowan unwrapped her legs and leaned against the cave wall.

"My mother gave it to me for my birthday why? And why did you stop?"

"Did she say where she bought it?"

"No. She said it was my fathers. What's the big deal?"

"Oh, my sweet minx you have no idea."

He had to figure out how to explain to her who she was, how vital she is without scaring her away. It seemed so easy when he played it out in his head, but now that he had felt just a glimmer of what she could do he didn't want to break their connection. He didn't want to share her. Amias began to pace.

Rowan reached out and grabbed his hand.

"Then perhaps you should fill me in because right now part of me wants to run and a stronger, more curious part doesn't want to leave until you fill me in. Which doesn't make any sense. I hardly know you yet I feel like I've known you forever."

"It makes perfect sense. Come sit with me and I'll try to explain."

Amias kissed the top of her hand leading her out into the night air.

The beach was now deserted. Sitting down on the sand Rowan drew her knees up to her chest and hugged them. The ocean breeze was stronger than earlier and she watched as it moved his long dark hair away from his face exposing a gentle, almost child-like expression.

Standing at the water's edge Amias took a deep breath, said a prayer to his Gods and began to tell her a tale.

"I think if I told you everything at once it would be too much to comprehend."

Amias was now sitting beside her. He did his best not to get distracted. But oh those lips! Focusing on the ocean waves Amias gathered his thoughts.

"Start small. I've got all night."

"Are you familiar with the story of the fountain of youth?"

"A little."

"You, Rowan, are that fountain of youth for our people."

Rowan began to laugh. "Yeah right..ya know what, if you wanted to be a buzz kill you won first prize."

"Do you really find it so hard to comprehend?"

"Yes I do. I believe that people have foolishly searched for something that doesn't exist. Hundreds of years wasted on a myth."

She started to stand up to take her leave but his firm hand grabbed her arm and pulled her back down. Laying her flat on her back and by placing a hand on either side of her Amias felt he could keep her from running off.

"I'm not joking Rowan. The sect that I belong to is dying off. We are centuries old. And with age, new diseases and climate change we can no longer reproduce successfully."

"You do realize you sound like a fucking fruit loop?"

"Yeah...it isn't easy to digest."

"What makes you think I can fix your sperm count?"

"Hear me out?"

"Go for it."

"It was written that a child conceived during an equinox and born during a solstice would hold the power to bring life, heal the body and unite her people."

"Sorry to disappoint but I am not one of your people."

"You're right you aren't JUST one of our people. You ARE our people."

"Nice try. I'm going to leave now. Good luck finding your fountain of youth."

Amias could feel her body begin to tense under him as she squirmed to free herself.

He needed to keep her there. So he did the only thing he could think of. He kissed her. Forcing his tongue into her sweet mouth and nudging her thighs apart he pressed his weight between them, leaving little room for her to escape.

He knew he should stop, that it was against sect law, but his heart and body said otherwise. Rowan was now moaning and reaching for his throbbing cock. The straps of her dress had fallen off her shoulders exposing her erect nipples. Oh, how her skin glowed in the moonlight. Kissing each one Amias convinced himself that one taste of her fountain was a just reward and no one would know.

He could feel her fingers entangled in his hair as she pushed his head down her stomach towards her open legs. The scent of her musk triggered the dormant animal inside him and with a quick slip of his right hand Amias pulled her panties to the side and plunged his warm tongue in between her pink flesh. He needed to go as deep as he could, he needed to feel her tremble, for her to feed him with her sweet nectar. He inserted one, then two fingers while still sucking on her clit. Rowan's hips moved to catch each wave of electricity that was being emitted from Amias's mouth. He could sense she was on the edge so he opened her wider, plunging his tongue even deeper and began to drink. Her orgasm filling his cup.

He knew he had to stop, her innocence wasn't his to take. She must remain intact. With one last lick Amias lifted his head and pulled away from the warmth of her body.

"Now it's my turn." Rowan moved to undo his buckle.

"Don't my sweet minx, we can't go any further." Pulling her hand away. "I've taken enough from your well."

"I don't understand. Don't you want me?"

"Of course I want you. That's the problem. I want all of you but you aren't mine to have."

"I don't see a problem."

"When I think of being with you I don't just think about a one nighter. I think of being deep within you. Staring into those luscious almond eyes as you take me in and tell me you only want me. Don't get me wrong, I want to have crazy sex with you but I also want to love you. Talking about what I want is mute, if the prince found out that I even stole a kiss from you I would be banished."

"Let's get one thing straight. I don't belong to anyone, not even a prince. And this story you made up to get me to fool around with you is fucked up. I would have without the lame story."

"Good to know....but I'm not making this up."

Rowan marched off towards the Kitchen Club tears of frustration began to puddle and fall down her face. What the hell is wrong with me? Pull it together girl, it's just your hormones being wonky. Like what the fuck?

Amias's figure faded away.

~ A storm is fast approaching

The wind blowing hard like waves of lust,

Hoping that they may soon reach you...

Taking us away

Drowning in tempestuous currents of gratification.

Now thunder, competing with the pulse of our hearts.

Lightning, electrifying our souls,

Flashing in time with our movements.....

Here comes the rain. ~

Rowan needed to stop moping. It had been a week since she left Amias on the beach and instead of chalking it up as just a weird but good time all she could do was overthink what he had told her. Could it be true? Could she really be so special that an entire population was dependent on her? And how is she supposed to help? What is the connection with her father?
Rowan needed answers and she was determined to get them.

Since Rowan's mom was away for the weekend she decided to roller-skate to the beach.
Ocean drive was busy. Scattered throughout the beach were vacationers slathered in coconut scented sunscreen, flipping occasionally trying to obtain the perfect tan. The haze of the day could be seen hovering just above the water. A few other skaters passed, one held a boom box and skated to the beat of Michael Jackson's "Wanna be Starting Something" and Rowan couldn't help but laugh to herself at the irony of the song.
Rolling to the end of the wooden bridge Rowan unlaced her skated and headed towards the rocks.
The white sand was deceiving. It looks so inviting, with its softness and sparkle, but as soon as she took a few steps it was hot. So hot she nearly ran to the waterline to avoid burning her soles.

Rowan walked the waterline toward what she hoped would be answers but when she reached the rocks only disappointment was there to meet her. All and any signs of Amias and the cave were gone. Skating to the nearest phone booth Rowen dialed Anna's number and then Tanya's. If she was going to shake this man from her head then she needed a distraction, a drink and to be with her friends.

It was pouring so hard when they arrived at the Kitchen Club they had to run to not get soaked. The place was packed and the cover band was playing a bad rendition of Motley Crue.

Rowan approached the bar while Anna and Tanya scanned the room for some hot guys.

"What's your poison?" a petite barmaid asked while placing three napkins down on the bar.

"I need a slow comfortable screw against the wall please."

"How many?"

"Three please."

"Only three? I'm sure I could give you more."

Rowan turned around to see who would drop such a pathetic line. And to her pleasant surprise it was her mystery dance partner from the other night. Rowan tried not to stare but damn, he was hot and those green eyes. What was up with the eye thing?

"Overly confident aren't you?"

Before he could respond Anna cut in to hand out their drinks and without breaking his gaze he lifted Rowan's hand to his lips, gently kissed it, disappearing into the crowd.

"What was that all about?" asked Tanya

"I have no idea but I'd like to find out."

Rowan's interest had been piqued. Taking several big sips of her drink, "Come on girls I didn't wear this leather dress for nothing. Let's dance!"

At first Rowan thought the overwhelming warmth had to do with dancing for so long. That the dizziness was due to the strobe lights and fog machine but when the chills started she knew she needed air so she headed toward the patio.

The heavy rain had turned into a warm drizzle. Standing out on the patio Rowan welcomed the quiet.

Leaning back against the wall, hidden in the shadows he watched her. Never had anyone gripped him or entranced him the way she did. He had never been chained in rhapsody. So, he stayed silent.

"I know someone's there. I can feel you."

She didn't turn around.

And he remained in the shadows. For a while.

Watching her tilt her face to enjoying the warmth of the watering sky, he slowly approached and when he could stay silent no more, he stood in her tranquility.

He had never been a man of many words. And right now no words were needed. He contemplated "willing" her to feel, to take note of all the sensations that were awakening in her. To help her feel the power she held, even nudging her undeviated desire towards him, but that would be fruitless. She needed to offer herself freely for it to materialize.

Rowan turned to face him.

"Stalk much?"

He said nothing.

"What's your name?"

He said nothing.

"The silent type huh? It doesn't matter. The way this night is going...you'll do."

Rowan took his hand, kissing each fingertip, drawing herself closer. She could smell the scent of sesame on his skin and scotch on his breath.

"Keelen. My name is Keelen."

"Keelen do you feel it? Do you feel that if you don't take in everything around you it will be lost?"

"Every waking hour."

Keelen searched her face. He wanted to worship her statuesque beauty, to reign in her desire. To be the one to set it free. It was becoming all too much. He could no longer contain himself and with time running out he picked her up and placed her in the nearest chair.

"Do I have your permission? Or doesn't it matter?"

"Permission granted...just don't tell me you're from Area 51. I've had enough weird encounters."

"I won't. I promise."

Keelen parted her legs and settled in between. He was in awe but too hungry to take his time. Without restraint he forced her mouth open with his darting tongue and she willingly met his with hers.

Keelen watched as she unzipped the front of her dress offering herself.

The rain fell harder, pooling on her stomach to quench his thirst as he continued to nibble his way down.

Stopping him. "Promise me you won't stop."

Keelen smirked. "Your wish is my command princess."

Settled on satisfying his promise Keelen tore her lace panties off and buried his tongue deep into her well, sucking and drinking all that she had to offer while circling her perfect little clit with his thumb.

Rowan pumped her hips vigorously against his mouth.

"Yes, that's it my princess....let go." Keelen continued to lick and dart his tongue simultaneous to the strokes of his fingers. He could taste her cycle turning. Soon she would be ready and he prayed the sect was right.

Clutching to the sides of the chair, a satisfying moan escaped Rowan and the heavens shook with her.

Keelen stood above her. His soul screamed a thousand "I love you's," but he needed to stay the course. She was his and it was time to take her home.

"Let's get you out of these wet clothes. Come with me."

Still in the flush of her newfound sensuality, Rowen readily took his hand. Snuggling into the curve of his arm as he guided her onto the beach and towards the rocks.

Rowan's senses had become heightened, as if something inside had been woken. Looking up at Keelen she could see his violet aura. The taste of salt on her lips was stronger and she could define, by scent, the different life forms wafting in from the ocean air.

When they reached the rocks the door was no longer there and in its place was a curtain of flowering jasmine.

"I don't understand," she said as she touched its petals, inhaling its strong fragrance.

"Did Amias not tell you?"

He began to position himself so she could see she wasn't in danger. Rowen had just opened her mouth to speak when Amias appeared.

"Ah! The guardian has arrived!" Keelen proclaimed.

Amias bowed then turned to Rowan. He wanted to explain. To tell her he can't get her out of his head. That without her silhouette he was blind.

"Why did he call you the guardian?"

Keelen broke in "You didn't tell her did you? Oh that's rich."

Keelen turned to Rowan, who was now getting annoyed at the secrecy.

"Amias here was appointed as your guardian the day you were born. To keep you safe and intact...then, when the sect could sense your awaking, to return you to me."

Keelen paused. Pivoted towards Amias "Now that wasn't so hard was it?"

Ah but alas...it was hard.

Amias was finding it difficult to separate his head and his heart. He wanted to put her on a pedestal, to keep her to himself but he knew her plight was bigger than himself.

"Amias is that true? Are you the reason why I have always felt like someone was watching me?"

Ignoring her questions Amias turned to Keelen.

"Why have you come?"

"Oh my faithful Amias, you were taking too long and as you know, I have little patience. And we have such little time. I figured I'd retrieve my betrothed myself."

"Wait, what?" Rowan's calm manner had cracked. "I don't know what the two of you have conjured up in your heads but I'm not waiting around to find out! And I'm not anyone's betrothed!"

The sand sifted harshly as she began to stomp off.

It was Amias who finally spoke. "Your father is waiting for you Rowan. Please come with us, hear him out. And if you want to return, no one will stop you."

"Tread lightly guardian, remember your place," Keelen quietly hissed in his ear.

Amid all the new sensations. The desire for two men and now information about her father thrown into the mix, things couldn't get any weirder. Throwing caution to the wind, Rowan followed them both into the cave.

The atmosphere in the cave had changed. The moss-covered floor was blooming with flowers. Jasmine was now growing on walls that were once bare. Fungi had sprung up along the walls edge, and, as if a light had been switched on, the quartz crystals shone brighter. Rowan walked slowly ahead of her escorts. She was in awe of this transformation. Keelen looked over at Amias giving him a knowing glare.

"Someone's been naughty." Keelen threw his arm around Amias's shoulder.

"It's not what you think sire."

"Oh, it's exactly what I think," Keelen said with a wink, then joined Rowan ahead.

Amias watched in silence as Keelen and Rowan took the lead. He knew the rules and he broke them. Did he feel remorse? No. He had waited all his life for a taste of her. Just to be alone in her presence was something he had wanted for the longest time. And now that she was about to find out her unlimited potential he didn't think he could summon the courage to leave her.

The walkway came to an end and opened up to a forest of trees. Rowan noticed that many of the trees and bushes were dying. Flowers were sparse and the smell of decay hovered. The sight of this made her heart hurt. Rowan wanted to stretch her arms around all that she saw and pull it into her bosom.

"I don't understand," she said, turning to Keelen. "Everything we just walked through was alive and beautiful. What has happened here?"

Again, Keelen turned around to Amias. "You really are lacking when it comes to details aren't you? Perhaps your tongue should do more than cause a flood."

Then directing his attention to Rowan, "You, my sweet woman made that cave come to life."

Keelen guided her out of the forest and in one sweeping hand gesture, "Can you imagine what you could do for your people?"

Rowan looked down into a valley where a village was tucked. She could see several houses, cobblestone paths, and what looked like a church carved in one of the mountains. There were no telephone poles or vehicles. No static or pollution in the air. It was as if she had stepped back in time before modern man had taken over.

"It's quite lovely but I feel as though everything is weeping. I can feel, and somehow, hear the pain."

Stepping up next to Rowan Amias pointed toward the sanctuary.

"That is where we will find your father, Vardon. He will explain all that is necessary."

Rowan's mother, Isleen, never told her her father's name and now she was about to put a face to it. Excitement to have someone pull all these story fragments together began to build.

"Well let's get this party started!" Keelen clapped, then headed down the path and to what he hoped would be a very fruitful evening.

Rowan found the stillness unnerving and she was beginning to get hungry.

"I suppose neither one of you happens to have a Whatchamacallit and a Tab? I haven't eaten and I really could use some food."

"We should be coming up to several apple trees soon. In the meantime here are some berries." Amias walked off the path and plucked a handful. Rowan ate from his hand. Pointing at the trees Amias spoke.

"According to ancient Gail, these Quicken trees were considered sacred. That they contained magical properties. It was told that the berries from these trees could reverse the aging process. For instance, an old woman of 99 could eat it and be restored to the age of 29."

Rowan stopped in mid chew, "Are you feeding me those berries?'

Keelen began to laugh and continued Amias's story.

"These trees were so special that they were guarded so that they would not be misused. This sacred tree has also been called by the name Rowan."

Popping the last of the berries into her mouth.

"I'm pretty sure my mother didn't name me after a tree."

"Maybe she didn't realize why she gave you that name, but just like the tree, you are the fountain and Amias is your guardian."

~ *The strokes from the brushes of your weird,*

Womanly charm

Has colored my life

And your smile breaks through the darkest of clouds ~

~ Chapter 5 ~

Keelen threw open the double wooden doors of the sanctuary. "Honey I'm home!!!"

"I'm not your honey," an older woman replied as she approached the three of them, stopping in front of Keelen and bowing.

Turning to Rowan. "We have been waiting a long time for you...and by the looks of you, I'm thinking you could use some fresh clothes and food."

Rowan immediately felt safe when she looked into the older woman's gray-blue eyes. Time had marked her face with lines, turned her long braided hair silver, but she was far from frail.

"That sounds wonderful, yes please. However, I would like to see my father."

"And you shall, but first things first."

Taking both of Rowans hands into hers, she led her down a stone hall that opened up into a bathhouse. Two young women were busy pouring oils of lavender and rose into the warm water.

"My name is Lady Una and these two are Nerifina and Freya. They will attend to all of your needs and wants. I will return later."

Nerifina and Freya began to remove Rowans dress. Her panties were long gone. Probably still sitting on the floor at the Kitchen Club. Her shoes somewhere in the sand. So there she stood buck naked like a jay bird, as the girls led her across the marble floor and into the copper tub.

Once emerged, Rowan watched as their indigo auras shimmered in the candle light.

Leaning back against the cold metal Rowan closed her eyes as Nerifina washed her hair.

Freya, still dressed in a blue cotton sheath, stepped into the water. It began as circular motions and ended in sighs. Freya massaged and washed her at the same time. Her hands moving up her thighs triggered a strong and steady vibration encouraging her nipples to harden and her velvet to throb.

Rowan wasn't sure she liked this "awakening." She had control issues and right now her desire had the wheel. It didn't matter if she was in the presence of man or woman, her eyes saw them as beautiful and her hands longed to heal.

Sitting up she reached out and pulled Freya closer. It came so naturally. The exploration with mouths, hands and tongues. Neither women shied away from Rowan's intentions, instead they gracefully fell into her trance, kissing her fully on the mouth. Nerifina lowered herself behind Rowan and began to rub essential oils onto her upper body. With her back against her chest, Rowan looked up to see her face and guided it towards hers, kissing her deeply. Freya had now separated Rowans long legs, placing one on either side of her shoulders, lifting her bottom. To an outsider the sight would have been seen as sexual, but to the people of the realm, Rowan was the elixher they needed to heal.

Nerifina lifted herself to the edge of the bath and willingly opened to Rowan's sweet pink tongue while Freya continued to feast from behind.

He watched for a while as the swan-like movements reached and searched, dipped and drank. It was an arousing sight but not just to his body but to the entire design.

Clearing his throat Keelen stepped forward with towel in hand. "The princess is not a tootsie-pop ladies, one last lick and go see to her dinner."

Keelen helped Rowan out of the tub and attempted to dry her off before Rowan could snatch the towel away. Grabbing the towel from his hands, she wrapped herself.

"Are you always this rude?"

"I have never thought myself to be rude. Witty and easily amused, yes, but never rude." Keelen had walked over to a large closet and opened up a robe of purple velvet for her. "So what was it like?"

Rowan attempted to be nonchalant as she allowed him to help her with the robe.

"I have no idea what you're talking about."

Keelen, still standing behind her, leaned into her ear wrapping his strong arms around her and dipping his hand between her thighs whispered, "To bring their womanhood back to life."

"I can't explain any of this," she said, spinning on her heels to face him. "I feel as though I'm on overload. All I want to do is touch and taste. It's crazy... all my senses are heightened. If I did drugs I'd swear I was high on a hallucinogen."

"That could pose a problem if you don't learn how to reign in that passion. I'm not in the habit of sharing."

Before she could respond Keelen signaled her to stop.

"You can daintily argue this at another time but right now let's get you clothed and fed."

Freya was waiting for them in the hallway, bowing as they approached.

"Freya will take you to your room and help you dress."

Then directing his next statement at the young woman.

"And just dress. Isn't that correct?"

Freya just kept her head down and led Rowan as fast as she could away from Keelens icy stare.

Her bedroom was much larger than her one at home. The stone walls were draped in tapestries, the floors covered in pelts, and to her right was a fireplace so big she could walk right into it. But what was so striking...sitting in the middle of the room, was a large bed. It wasn't just any bed, the headboard was a carved Rowen tree with its branches extending outward, creating a canopy of green. The bedding was of the same fabric and Rowan found it all so welcoming. If it wasn't for her growling stomach she surely would have welcomed sleep.

Freya helped her into a gown of black velvet and began randomly placing babies' breath in her hair. Rowan admired the gown, how it laid open to her navel, exposing all but her breasts.

"I'm not sure this is the right attire to be meeting my father for the first time."

Amias stood in the hallway watching her from a distance. He had just gotten an earful from Keelen and needed to tread lightly.

"You look stunning." Amias entered the room, stopping just inside the door.

"I still find this all unbelievable and I'm sure my mother has tried to call me. She is going to be worried sick."

"Don't fret your mother won't even notice. Time is much different here. Come, I will walk you to the dining hall."

Rowan noticed that he too had dressed for dinner. He was no longer wearing the style of the 80's but was dressed in brown leather pants and a white linen shirt.

Amias began to make small talk to keep from stealing a kiss.

"The entire village is buzzing about your arrival and are preparing for your banquet. They have been waiting a very long time for their Goddesses blessings."

Amias's words laid heavy on her mind. She wasn't sure how to live up to such expectations. Everything was so bizarre yet she felt in harmony with this new found land.

When they reached the dining-hall Keelen was standing in front of a large fireplace drinking and laughing with several other men. There were lit torches hanging on the walls and a wheel of candles extended front the ceiling. The table was low and flanked with long benches. The only chairs sat at each end, and they too, were carved like a Rowan tree, with branches extending outward forming the arms. Hearing them enter Keelen turned to greet her.

"Ah! You finally decided to grace us with your presence."

Striding across the room Keelen stopped in front of Amias, reaching out smoothing a crease in his shirt.

"I was afraid Amias's thirst was getting the better of him."

Lady Una was now there shaking her head and rolling her eyes.

"Ignore him. He isn't always such a prick."

Keelen started laughing. "Ahhh, but I do have one that prose will be written about."

Lady Una joined in the laughter. "You mean myths." Still laughing to herself Lady Una led Rowan to the table.

"Don't let Keelens arrogant nature bother you, it's really just a front. And I would know. I have been his teacher since his birth. I also know what's in his britches and his heart. There is no malice in that man."

Rowan watched as several people began bringing in platters of food, a hot stew and baskets of bread.

"You look so anxious dear." Lady Una reached for a pitcher and began to pour herself and Rowan a drink.

Handing her one of the silver goblets. "It will help."

"What is it?"

"Well. It's believed that it offers immortality to humans and a sacred state of bliss for the Gods."

Patting Rowans hand she leaned in and whispered, "It's just water and fermented honey."

Lady Una rose giving her a knowing wink, then announced it was time to eat.

There was something about the strength Keelen exuded that made Rowan think he would be a good candidate to sire many healthy offspring. "Oh my God, what the hell am I thinking?" she whispered to herself, "snap out of it."

"Dreaming of our wedding night?"

Keelen bit into a fig and took the chair at the other end of the table.

Ignoring his comment. "Where is my father?

"He will be joining us after we've dined."

Both of his feet were now on the table. Drinking the fermented honey Keelen never took his eyes off her.

The food smelled amazing and Rowan was famished.

Kindly declining the venison stew that was set before her. "I don't eat meat, but thank you."

"You should try the fish, it's much better than what you are used to." Amias handed her a plate of battered bluegill, steamed carrots and asparagus.

"Why is it better?"

"Unlike the modern world, our bodies of water are free of pollutants. All its life form is pure."

"This I have to try."

 In union, everyone bowed their heads, clinked their glasses and began to eat.

Rowan was relieved that the conversations during dinner didn't include her. She was beginning to feel like a spectacle to be gawked at and she'd much rather focus her attention on the deliciousness of the food. So much food.

When the dishes were being cleared, bowls of berries and cream took their places. Keelen rose from his chair. "I want to thank all who prepared this fine meal but dessert will have to wait. I would like a private moment with Rowan before Vardon steals her away."

Without a murmur the entire room cleared and Amias closed the heavy doors behind him.

Rowan remained seated. It was her time to lean back and put her feet on the table. With a body full of sustenance, her strength of will returned and she was beginning to feel in control.

"Okay peacock or should I say My Lord? Yes... I like the way that rolls off my tongue... it's sexy. What is it you want?"

Her changed demeanor made her even more desirable to him. He wanted to throw her on the table and make her the banquet.

"I just wanted to be in your presence without the noise. Is that too much to ask?"

Rowen relaxed and allowed him to fill her cup. She was clearly enjoying the drink. It made her feel warm and floaty.

"I'm sorry I didn't mean to sound so harsh." Taking a sip she licked her lips and asked him to kiss her.

"Only if I can kiss your sexy knees and nibble you all over afterwards." Rowan teasingly pulled up her gown exposing her knees.

"Do with me what you will my lord, I am here for your nibbling." Keelen could taste the honey on her tongue as he passionately kissed her. Holding her head with one hand and stroking her face with the other Rowan began to undo his leather pants.

He didn't stop her this time, instead his hardness welcomed the softness of her small hands. Pushing him back against the table she removed his shirt while making sure her lips never left his body.

He watched as she deliberately ran her tongue down his tight abs, lightly biting his hips as she lowered his pants. His heart was racing, skipping a beat when his eyes locked with hers as she took him fully into her mouth.

Rowens desire to satisfy him became an intense sensation. Grabbing his firm ass she guided him with long sucking strokes. She could hear his low moans and smiled to herself as he held her hair back so he could watch as she pumped him faster.

He was doing his best to hold back until she ordered him to feed her. Then all self-control was lost with the sweetest release.

Refusing to let the moment fade Keelen pulled her up and laid her down on the table.

"I believe you own me some knee nibbling."

"Be my guest." Rowan pulled up her gown offering her knees.

Keelen planted quick soft kisses on each but what he wanted was more of the world that lay hidden between her thighs.

Pulling the chair closer to the table's edge Keelen sat and began dining on the sweetest of desserts.

When they were done feasting off of each other, and he on his back, and she wrapped in his arms, Keelen finally knew what it was like to feel complete.

~ Leave me not,

I've wandered this world

For so long,

In search for you ~

~ Chapter 6 ~

Standing at the table where they laid, Lady Una cleared her throat. Waking Keelen.

"Yes?" Turning his face towards her.

"I'm going to assume you behaved yourself."

"Why do you think so little of me and my ability to restrain myself?"

"Because I know you and I know the power she possesses has yet to be harnessed."

"Ye of little faith...if it was anyone else I'd be offended."

"Vardon is waiting for her in the gardens."

"Tell Vardon she will be there soon."

Lady Una took her orders and left.

****

Rowan smiled with eyes closed.

The cool night air was perfumed with the mix of Evening Primrose and Wisteria. She watched as the fireflies danced around her, welcoming her into the garden.

"I've waited a long time for this moment."

Rowan couldn't see where the voice was coming from. She began walking further into the garden until she spotted a vine of grapes. Under it stood her father. A broad man with a gentle face and hair of red.

Mind don't fail me now. She had rehearsed what she would say but when she opened her mouth nothing came. She was speechless. Vardon pointed to one of the trees.

"Can you hear the nightingale? She's singing for you." His voice was deep.

"Why me? Why did you choose to make me? Rowan's voice began to crack.

"I didn't make you. The Gods chose you. They knew you would be our hope for life and could put balance back into this world."

"No offense but I highly doubt the Gods made you sleep with my mother and then leave her."

Rowan was determined to not let him off the hook no matter what tale he spun.

"What happened between your mother and I can be discussed at another time. What you need to understand is that I was sent to her. The Gods knew that it was her that would birth the mother of this new earth. Do you not feel your attachment to all living things? Do you not see life bloom where once there was none? And to think, you have yet to reach your full potential."

Vardon relaxed his body. He knew for her to process it all it had to be given to her in small doses.

"Come sit with me."

Rowan joined him on the stone bench. Her fingers fidgeting with her choker.

"Why did you give this to my mother?"

"First let me say your mother is one of the most beautiful women I have ever laid eyes on. She made my heart sing as I watched her flutter from one thing to another and it crushed me when I had to go. But the necklace, that's not mine. It was a gift for you from the King."

"Why would a king give this to me when I wasn't even conceived yet? And why does Keelen have the same one?"

"Keelen has one because that is his family's crest."

"Please don't tell me... he's a relative."

Vardon laughed, "You can relax, and you two are not related. However, you are betrothed to him."

"So I've heard...but what makes you think I want to marry him or anyone for that matter?"

"You will."

 "If I am the Goddess that has the ability to bring life back to your people why on earth would I listen to the commands of other Gods?"

Vardon took a deep breath. He wanted to be able to explain the intricacies of what was to come and what will be, but right now he knew she had to stand her ground and burn off some steam before she could open up and welcome her responsibilities.

"Once your story is fully told you will understand."

Rowen stood up crossing her arms in front of her.

"Then tell me."

Vardon rose. "It's getting late my dear, we can continue this at another time."

Rowan watched as Vardon walked away leaving her there... alone, again.

Keelen found her crying under the grapevine. Immediately he wanted to rush to her side, to comfort her, but it would hurt him more if she rejected him. So he sat on the ground in front of her.

"I take it didn't go as you planned?"

Wiping her face with the back of her hand. "I don't even know why I'm so upset. It's not like I know the man. I just thought he would be a little more excited to see me, perhaps even hug me."

Keelen started placing daisies in between her toes.

"Vardon is a scholar and comes from a very priestly class of people. His emotions are well hidden. He will reveal himself in time."

Rowan's smile was faint. "Do you really think I have the ability to change things?"

"Yes I do. Let me show you something."

Keelen got up and started searching. When he returned he had a stick in one hand and a bowl of muddy water in another.

Sitting back down him placed the bowl in her lap.

"Now, I want you to place your fingers into the bowl."

Rowan followed his direction.

"Close your eyes and picture clean water."

She wasn't sure what he was up to but this night couldn't get any stranger. Trying to clear her mind, Rowan took in the evening air and exhaled. She pictured she was sweeping up oil slicks in the ocean, dragging nets across the bottom of lakes and scooping up garbage the world had dumped. With those images in mind she felt a vibration in her fingertips.

"Now open your eyes."

Keelan was sitting there looking like a child on Christmas morning. The bowl of water was now clear.

"I did that?"

"Wait...there's more."

 Keelen took away the bowl and placed a stick in her hands.

"I want you to think about life, about someone that you love and watch what you can do."

Again, she took in the night air and exhaled. To her delight she watched as the stick slowly grew branches. Leaves unraveled, buds appeared and eventually the buds blossomed.

He was now kneeling in front of her.

"You did this and you have the ability to do so much more. Now do you understand how important you are to our people? To the world?"

Rowan's fear of the unknown was replaced with curiosity. Not just about her abilities but about him.

"What about you? Am I important to you?"

Keelens heart skipped a beat. "More than you'll ever know."

Rowan wasn't sure if she was falling in love with him or if her feelings for him had to do with her powers but at that moment it didn't matter. Keelen had come to comfort her, to raise her spirits and make her smile and that was enough for now. She wrapped her arms around his neck and hugged him, snuggling into the nape of his neck, lightly kissing it.

He wanted to protect her from all that he could. To be the one lifting her out of the darkness and to walk beside her as her husband. If only his fear of rejection would stop getting in the way, keeping his heart silent.

Rowan's light kisses became more direct and firmer. Pulling up her dress she straddled herself on his lap, allowing him access to her breasts. Tenderly, he took each one in his mouth, lightly biting her nipples. Keelen placed one hand on her back to hold her as she arched, and with the other, he guided her ass in a rocking motion against his hardness.

The garden air was intoxicating. Every bud and every sleeping flower began to wake in sync to their passion and the fruits began to ripen. Keelen opened his eyes to watch her mouth as his fingers danced in her wetness only to stop when he noticed Lady Una standing near the arbor.

"You do realize you have the worst timing?"

Keelen lifted Rowan off his lap and helped her up.

"I think my timing is perfect. Rowan needs her rest and from what I can see you could use a cold bath."

Rowan giggled and followed Lady Una out of the garden but not before running back and kissing him on the lips.

Keelen continued to stand there taking in the phenomenal display nature had unveiled because of their passion.

"You can come out now," he ordered.

Amias appeared from behind a tree.

"You really need to break this habit."

Amias said nothing.

Keelen, now positioned in front of him. "I believe it is time to release you from your duties when it comes to Rowan. Don't fret she is in very good hands...mine."

Amias wanted to say something as Keelen was leaving but he held his tongue. It would do no good. It's futile to argue with a demi-god, especially one on a mission.

       Rowan sat there listening to the crackling of the fire and watched as its shadows danced in an orange glow.   She could feel sleep creeping in as Lady Una helped her into bed.
"Lady Una I just wanted to tell you how much I appreciate you. You've been so kind."
Lady Una pushed the hair out of Rowan's eyes and smiled, then sat down next to the fire and began to sing a lullaby.
"That's lovely." Rowen yawned trying to fight her eyelids from closing.
"I used to sing this when Keelen was a babe. Perhaps one day I will sing it to yours."
 Rowan never heard Lady Una's last words; she was already drifting off to sleep.

~ Someday, our plight will bloom

Children will run

In that golden afternoon...

Till' then, under a blanket of stars

When the night is quiet,

And natures ours

We'll scatter seed

Wish upon the moon ~

Rowan was startled awake with Freya rushing into her room, jumping on the bed and hugging her so tight she could hardly catch her breath.

"Oh my goodness! Freya what is going on?"

Freya was giddy. "I'm just so happy and it's all because of you!"

Rowan's mind wandered as she sat quietly listening to Freya.

She missed her friends. She missed hanging out with them, listening to records and talking about boys. She missed her mom's laugh and the smell of her hair and the way she would use her paintbrushes to hold it up.

Rowan forced a smile.

"I don't understand."

"I'm finally with child!"

"That's wonderful! I'm so happy for you."

Rowan hugged her again. "I really don't understand. How do I have anything to do with it?"

"You healed my womb silly!"

"That's enough. Freya, get off Rowan and go tend to her breakfast."

Lady Una ordered as she walked in the bedroom with fresh clothes.

Freya got up giving Rowan one last hug then ran off to gather fresh eggs.

"Is what she told me true Lady Una?"

"That she's pregnant? Yes." Lady Una started stoking the fire to get the chill out of the air.

"No...The healing of her womb."

Lady Una stopped, pausing for a moment to add more kindling.

"Yes dear you healed what was needed to continue life."

Rowan wrapped herself in a blanket and stood before the fire watching it dance. Had she really helped Freya? And if so, what was it she did to make it happen?

"Would you like me to send in Nerifina to help you dress dear?"

"No thank you I can do it myself."

Lady Una quietly closed the doors behind her and left Rowan in her thoughts.

A knock on the door startled her. Lady Una had returned holding a wooden tray of fruits, honey, and porridge. Placing it on the dressing table she motioned Rowan to sit while she brushed and plaited her hair.

"Will I be seeing my father today?"

"He's been very busy with those in the village preparing for the ceremonial banquet that will be taking place tomorrow night but I will tell him that if he is as wise as he says, then he should pay you a visit."

Finishing off the fruit, Rowen walked over to the vast mirror that leaned against the wall to the left of the bed. It resembled the large floor to ceiling mirror that stood at the bottom of the stairs back home. Looking at her reflection she wondered if Keelen saw her as a woman he could love or just a Goddess he could possess.

"You seem lost in thought are you alright dear?"

"I'm so confused. I have all these feelings for Keelen. It's like I have a tug-of-war going on inside me. And then I think of Amias."

Lady Una began dabbing rose oil behind Rowans her ears and wrists. "Keelen is a good man, much different than his father. And when he loves, he loves deeply. The two of you are more alike than you know. As for your guardian Amias, you should shake that man out of your head. He has demons not even you can heal."

Placing a kiss on Rowan's cheek, "Come with me, your anxious suitor awaits."

Stepping out into the corridor Rowan could see him pacing and mumbling to himself.

She found the sight of his vulnerability appealing and arousing. He was wearing a shirt in the same shade of blue as her dress. She wondered; had he done it on purpose? His hair was held back with a leather strap but because he kept running his hands over it, a few stray locks fell against his chiseled face.

"Have I kept you long?" Leaning up and kissing his cheek.

Keelen placed a chain of black-eyed susans on top of her head.

"You are worth the wait." Returning her kiss fully on her mouth, biting her bottom lip before releasing.

"I thought you would like to get away from this place and accompany me on my duties."

"Oh I would really like that. I was beginning to get claustrophobic."

Stepping outside and into the morning air several men on horses, pulling a large cart, stopped in front of them. Keelen greeted each one and began feeding an apple to one of the horses, handing another to

Rowan, for her to do the same. He watched for a moment as she playful talked and caressed the horses.

"I just love them Keelen! They are so strong and majestic. I just want to give them big hugs." And she did.

"Should I be jealous?" he said jokingly.

"Well if you are...perhaps you'll need to step up your game."

Rowan walked over and peered into the cart.

"What is all this for?"

Lifting some of the items he explained.

"Once a month I, with the help of others, go into the center of the village and distribute food, honey, and other wares to the people."

"So you're like Robin Hood, steal the from the rich and give to the poor...without the stealing part."

"Hardly, the people here work hard and most things are done with a bartering system. But there are some who don't have items that they can spare, or to barter."

"I wish the world was like this. I think what you're doing is honorable. And...You might have just scored some brownie points."

The day couldn't have gone any better. Rowan was finding so much joy handing out the contents of the wagon and meeting the people from the village. She chose to ignore her sense of being watched. Instead, she and Keelen listened to their stories, welcomed their embraces, and when the cart was empty they continued their day with a walk through the market.

Throughout the day she was greeted by people who repeatedly told her how much they had prayed to the Gods for her arrival, offering her gifts of flowers, oils and different dyed linen.

With twilight quickly approaching Keelen wanted to show her one last thing. Directing the horsemen to ride ahead to the destination, he offered Rowan his hand, leading her out of the village and to the edge of a bluff.

Looking out Rowan's soul swooned. There before her, was a river that ran between them and a mountain of trees. And in those trees, a path that led to a castle whose banners held the Celtic symbol she now wore around her neck.

He searched her face hoping she saw the future he had dreamed about, the one that included her.

Rowan's eyes never left the beautiful landscape.

"Is this your home?"

"Yes. One day I hope you would think of it as yours as well."

 Keelen held his breath waiting for her response. He knew if time wasn't running out he would wait a thousand lifetimes for her. She made him feel as though he had a higher purpose, that what he did was worthy and when she looked at him, she only saw him, the man, not the person he was born or raised to be.

She continued to watch as the Blue Heron dived in and out of the water and the fluttering of a Monarch butterfly while contemplating her response.

Her silence was tearing at his heart. He knew he need not rush her reply.

Hoping to prompt her in her decision. "Some say that a monarch is a sign that one is on their right path in life."

Rowan felt good with what she was about to tell him. She was confident that she was on the right path, her path, and no one, not even the Gods were going to stand in her way.

Sitting him down next to her she could see how terrified he was. Figuring she needed to ease his fears she climbed onto his lap and brushed the hair from his face.

"These feelings I have for you and all that has happened is overwhelming and it scares me. And when I'm alone I'm so afraid that I will turn around and you will no longer be there. I can't promise that I won't want to touch or taste others but what I can promise is that I will work on other ways to love, to heal and nurture those around me. I surrender myself to you not because it's my duty, not because the Gods planned it, but because my soul has been screaming a thousand "I love you's" since the day your lips fell upon mine."

With each and every word that fell from her mouth, Keelen felt as if the weight of the world had been lifted. And when she finished he covered her face with kisses until her mouth found his.

He didn't care that the sky was now littered with stars or that the air was becoming cool. All he cared about was her. Keelen continued to kiss her, biting softly on her lower lip, basking in its sweetness. Then kissing her perfect jawline he proceeded down her dainty chest then back to her mouth, pulling away only to whisper "I love you."

As they undressed one another Rowan had never felt so free. Her naked body fit perfectly surrounded by nature and as he laid her down on the soft grass it felt as if the ground was her cradle.

"Are you sure?" he asked

"Quite sure my Lord."

Keelen watched as she slowly parted her legs so he could see that which delighted him. He didn't think he could get any harder but when she started to part her velvet and he could see the wetness on her fingers, he dropped to his knees. Lifting her hips to his mouth he vigorously began darting his tongue in and out. Stopping only to suck on her clit. From the sweat that was forming on her skin and the rhythmic tightening of her delicate walls, he knew she was on the edge. Moving his body upward he separated her velvet lips with his engorged head, rubbing it around her entrance. Slowly pushing the tip of his cock in and then pulling it back out. It was her first time and he knew the girth of his manhood could easily cause pain.

Rowan was growing impatient. She wanted him and she wanted him now. Pulling herself up her pushed Keelen on his back, covered his mouth with hers and lowered herself, covering his tower with her nectar. She felt a sharp pain at first but it immediately faded into a pulsation of desire.

Rowan arched her back moaning with pleasure as she rubbed her clit and moved herself up and down, hugging the thickness of his manhood.

He loved watching as her beautiful pussy eagerly, though gradually, swallowed and enveloped his pumping shaft. He was having a hard time holding back when her body began to send a vibration through his. He watched her face flush as he burst with sheer bliss filling her with his seed.

Keelen continued to hold her in his arms as her trembling eased. Reaching for his leather pouch he pulled out a gold ring and slipped it on her finger.

Rowan admired it. Holding her hand out so she could see the design and stones in the moonlight.

"How long have you been keeping this from me?"

"Not long. I had it made specifically for you. Don't you like it?"

"It's breathtaking and fits perfectly."

Kissing her. "We fit perfectly."

"Yes we do."

Rowan was starting to become aroused again but before she could satisfy her need Keelen wisely suggested they continue their lovemaking away from mosquitoes.

Riding in the back of the wagon, as the horseman carried them to the sanctuary, Keelen explained the meaning of each stone in her ring.

"The Opal in the middle represents Ops, a Goddess of fertility. The two flanking stones are Amber, which contain a healing property, and the next two are Obsidian, for protection."

Rowen held her hand out to admire it again.

"You really put a lot of thought into this. I love it and I love you."

Entwined in the warmth of furs a new life was created under the light of the moon.

~ You brought me back to a place in time

Where life was as easy as addition, and

Complete like my grandmother's dishes.

In your eyes I see myself,

Feeling, reaching, touching

For perfect harmony ~

~ Chapter 8 ~

Keelen had been watching Rowan sleep when she opened one eye.

"How long have you been staring at me?

"I can't help it. I'm just in awe with you and the fact that you love me makes me want to scream it from the hilltops."

Snuggling closer to him under blankets of green Rowan rested her head on his chest and began playing with the soft hair that covered his upper body.

"If you keep doing that we will never leave this bed." Pulling her naked body on top of his.

"Sounds like a plan to me," guided him into her warmth.

Rowan enjoyed all the intimacy she had encountered but to her, there was no better feeling than feeling his hardness reach her where there is no return.

Moving his hands down her back, Keenen took pleasure in the fluidity of their moving bodies, like a Waltz of passion. His hands cupped the base of her ass so that his fingers could play while she guided herself up and down his hard cock.

The sounds she made when he was pleasing her drove Keelen crazy. Covered her mouth with his, he could taste the deliciousness of her tongue. Inserting his fingers he began to pound his cock harder and faster, escalating her orgasm until she screamed her release and he, catching it with kisses.

Without knocking Lady Una walked into the bedroom carrying fresh clothes and stopping at the foot of the bed. Trying not to move a sleeping Rowan off him, Keelen propped one arm under his head.

"This time Lady Una your timing was off."

"I'm afraid to disappoint you my Lord, but the entire sanctuary could hear your "timing." Now get up. There are many things to be done before the ceremony and you are needed at council."

"I think you enjoy bossing me around."

Keelen woke Rowan. Explained he would soon return, planted a kiss on top of Lady Una's head and left feeling like a new man.

Lady Una, now directing her attention to Rowan.

"I have a feeling you've worked up quite an appetite. I'll have your ladies bring you some breakfast. Is there anything else you need before we begin getting you ready?"

"I'd like to take my breakfast out in the gardens if that's alright."

"Of course it is my dear."

Lady Una noticed the ring that adorned Rowan's hand and smiled.

"I see you said yes."

"Oh Lady Una I am so very happy!"

Rowen threw her arms around Lady Una and hugged her before she closed the doors behind her.

Out in the garden Freya and Nerifina laid out a blanket, cushions and food. Rowan finally felt at peace. No longer was there a constant buzzing in her veins or disbelief in who she was and what her powers could do. Laying back, she closed her eyes welcoming the warmth of the sun and thoughts of the night before.

From where he stood he could see her naked form through her sheath. He knew time was running out and if he didn't take charge of the situation now he may never have the opportunity.

He walked over and stood in front of her, blocking the sun. Her legs were bent and he could see between them, causing a stirring in his loins.

Without opening her eyes.

"You make a terrible window, could you please move."

Amias knelt down. He wanted to drink from her, to run his tongue over every inch of her body but that thought quickly slipped away when Rowan opened up her eyes and immediately sat up.

"I didn't mean to startle you. I just thought maybe you'd like to go back home and get a few things. Perhaps see your mother before the festivities this evening."

"I can do that?"

"What can she do Amias?" Keelen made himself comfortable beside her.

Rowan turned to Keelen, "Amias was just saying he could take me home so I could see my mother and have me back in time for the ceremony."

"Did he? How thoughtful of you but unfortunately the veil between our worlds has closed and only I or Rowan can open it."

Surprised by what he was hearing Amias began to pace.

"I don't understand...the veil isn't supposed to close until..." His face became red with rage.

"Until what dear brother?" Keelen said as he took a bite of melon.

"Brother?" Rowan peeped.

"Ah yes my love, Amias here is my half-brother. We share the same father."

Furious that Keelen had stolen something else that he felt was rightly his, stormed off into the sanctuary leaving Keelen there to gloat.

Rowan fed Keelen another piece of melon. "What's his damage?"

"His what?"

"His problem... I don't understand."

"Amias has a darkness in him. I was hoping your grace and nurturing personality would have changed him."

Keelen began to caress her face. "Fret not, he is no longer your guardian."

"Keelen, will you promise me that you will take me to see my mother? I miss her and I only think it's proper if she knows what's going on."

Lightly kissing her lips. "Anything for you".

Rowan kissed him back, teasing him by tracing her tongue across his lips. "MMMmmmmm, you continue to do that and we will...".

Just then Lady Una appeared quite flushed in the face.

"You just can't get enough of me can you Lady Una?"

Bowing. "There's no time for witty banter my Lord, Vardon needs to speak with you NOW!"

"Fine. Rowan my sweet, we can pick this up later."

After Keelen left the garden, Lady Una began to help Rowan pick up. She wondered what could be so important and why the urgency. She tried to direct her thoughts about the coming event but she had a strange feeling something bad was about to happen.

"Lady Una what does my father want with Keelen?"

"He just needs to go over some last minute details."

"Why do I feel as though you are leaving something out?"

Lady Una didn't want to frighten Rowan but she knew if she didn't warn her, then the visions Vardon had seen may come true.

"All I can say is that you need to be wary of Amias. Do not let yourself be alone with him and no matter what he tells you, he's twisting the truth."

"Why would he lie to me? He's been my guardian since my birth and he brought me here."

"Amias is full of jealousy. At first, he intended to return you to your people but once he drank from you, his own desire for you, and for power, changed him back to the man he once was... before you. He had no intention to bring you here. That is why Keelen showed up when he did."

Bringing a smile to her face, Lady Una wrapped one of her arms around Rowen, "That's enough negative talk. Let's go and get you prepared."

****

Keelen stood in the council chambers admiring the beauty of the round table and what it represented. In the center a Celtic symbol was carved, each end, representing the four elements, and along the edge, carvings depicting the twelve zodiacs. He grew excited at the idea that soon, Rowan would be sitting here with him, sharing the same idea for their people.

"Oh good your here," Vardon said as he threw open the double doors followed by nine other members.

Taking a seat Keelen gestured for them to do it as well.

"So what is so dire that it couldn't wait until tomorrow?"

Vardon spoke first. "We have been crying, my Lord and the Gods have shown us that something ominous is about to occur. We need to take precautions for your and Rowans safety."

Keelen bowed his head and began to rub his temples.

"And did the Gods show you who or what this threat is?"

An older priestess spoke next.

"I'm afraid my Lord that Amias's darkness has returned and he may succeed this time."

Keelen stood to address them.

"We do not know that it was Amias. He willingly stepped down as a warrior to redeem and repent. Is that not what an honorable man would do? Yes, I agree, he is becoming too invested in Rowan. That's why I relieved him from his duties."

Pushing his chair away from the table, Vardon was trying to find the right words without upsetting all those who looked to him for wisdom.

"No disrespect Keelen, but not all men can be redeemed. Amias is a bitter man. He feels he is the one entitled to take your fathers seat as King, and because of that, he should have the Goddess Rowan!"

"Calm yourself Vardon. Amias is but a mortal man. He cannot heal our people and land. He cannot create a child with powers to do so. The people know this and would not support his reign."

This was not how Keelen wanted to be spending his day but Amias had been acting odd of late and his lurking...well...perhaps the council was right.

"So what does this council suggest?"

Vardon exhaled with relief. "We believe, until the ceremony is over, Amias should be held in his quarters with guards outside his door. Then afterwards, be sent on a pilgrimage and only return when the Gods have spoken."

Without breaking his stare with Vardon, Keelen shouted to the guards to find Amias and bring him to the counsel. Then directed one of the priestesses to go check on Rowan.

Keelen was pacing when the guards returned empty handed.

"Well? Where is he?"

"I'm sorry my Lord, but he is nowhere in the sanctuary."

Furious, Keelen ordered the guards to search the grounds. How he could have been so naive, he thought to himself. He needed to inform his people about the safety of their future Queen.

Rowan felt like she was in a fairy-tale. Freya and Nerifina tended to bathing and rubbing essential oils into her skin. Using crushed berries, they added color to her cheeks and lips. Rowan had a hard time refraining from licking it off because it tasted so good. Standing on a small stool and facing the full-length mirror Rowan watched as several women made final Celtic stitches on the hem of her gown. It was a beautiful shade of pale blue with bell sleeves, a low waist, and a deep vee neckline. A braided rope of leather sat around her waist. A pouch of gemstones, for good luck was attached. When finished, Lady Una sat Rowan down and began braiding ribbons and wildflowers into her hair.

Her entire bedroom was so full of excitement that Rowan didn't notice the Priestess enter until she started whispering in Lady Una's ear. Lady Una nodded along with whatever was being said and Rowan could see her force a smile.

Something wasn't right, she felt off.

"Lady Una is everything okay?"

"Yes, everything will be okay. Just a little hiccup."

"What kind of hiccup? And before you start, remember I can tell when you are hiding something."

"The council is concerned about Amias and they decided it's best to keep an eye on him. They just need to find him first."

Lady Una began studying Rowan's face. "Are you feeling alright dear? You look flushed."

"Honestly, no. I'm feeling lightheaded."

Lady Una walked Rowan over to the bed and assisted her out of her gown.

"Maybe you just need to rest for a spell."

Helping her get comfortable Lady Una reached for the pitcher of water noticing the bowl of berries. The same berries that were used on Rowan's lips.

"Freya, Nerifina, where did you get those berries?

Nerifina stepped forward. "Amias brought them in. He said Lord Keelen sent them."

Lady Una grabbed the nearest piece of cloth, dipped it in the water and started removing the berry stain from Rowan's lips and cheeks.

"Don't just stand there girls! Go get the healer now!"

Lady Una sat on the bed and continued to dab Rowan's brow.

"I need you to do something for me. I need you to use your gifts and fight whatever poison Amias put on those berries."

Rowan started to nod off when Keelen ran into the room followed by the healer. Then dropping to his knees next to the bed, he wept.

"This is all my fault. I should have never given Amias the benefit of the doubt. I should have been here protecting you."

Rowen smiled through sleepy eyes. "Don't blame yourself."

There was a loud clap of hands. "I need the room cleared. Please ...out in the hallway...and that includes you too my Lord," ordered the healer.

Keelen wanted to protest but he knew he would have to deal with Lady Una's wrath if he did.

In the corridor a priestess was praying with Freya and Nerifina. Vardon was shouting orders to guards while Keelen sat on the floor with his back against a stone wall, never taking his eyes off the door. Lady Una could see the pain in Keelens face. Bending down and lifting his chin, "You are not to blame. Now stop this worry and start focusing on her. Use your gifts. The Gods didn't give you them so you could waste them. Focus and all will be well."

When the healer was done tending to Rowan, she stepped out to address the situation with the crowd that had formed outside her door.

Bowing, "My Lord, you can ease your mind. Rowan will recover. The berries intent was not to kill her. The mixture of herbs on them was to cause only sleep."

Keelen turned to Vardon. "I suggest you best start scrying and find out what the hell my brother is up to!"

Following Keelens orders Vardon quickly called the other members of the council and disappeared deep into the sanctuary.

Lady Una ordered the rest to go about their duties and followed Keelen as he hurried to Rowans side.

"My Lord, you look as though the heavens have stolen years from your face. Come kiss me and let me renew you."

Keelen pulled her up into his strong arms and did what she asked. He never wanted to stop kissing her, holding her. She was now his world and serving her, his greatest honor.

"How are you feeling?"

"I'm much better." Rowan leaned back against the pillows. "Your healer is very nice but from now on I want my mother. So...you need to figure something out."

"I thought you said you were fine? Why would you need your mother?"

"All children need their mothers." Turning to Lady Una, "Or mother figures."

Keelen smiled, "Yeah... Lady Una is a keeper."

Lady Una smiled back, kissed Keelen on the cheek and left the room.

Rowen, feeling more like herself as the minutes passed, climbed into Keelens lap.

"What do you plan on doing about Amias?" Lightly tracing his lips with her finger.

"Do you really want to know what I have planned or would you rather take advantage of this moment alone?"

Rowan placed one knee on each side of him so that he was eye level with her navel and lifted off her nightdress in one swoop.

"Both."

Keelen watched as good bumps appeared on her body as he ran his hands over its entirety. He began to kiss her sides, her breasts. He loved the fullness of her ass, the curve of her hips, and the strength in her thighs. Gazing at her perfect form he promised himself that he would always love her as if it was his last.

Rowan lowered herself, then rotated her body so she back was resting on his, sliding her velvet down on his hard cock. Keelen watched in the full length mirror as Rowan rocked her hips, pumping harder and harder. And when her heavy breathing turned into moans, Keelen lifted her up, put her on all fours in front of the mirror and started thrusting deeper.

Rowan could feel the heat rise to her chest, her face. She knew her climax was near, "Harder my Lord, harder!"

Keelen moved his hands from her hips to her ass, spreading her farther apart so he could watch his cock appear then disappeared inside her. Simultaneously reaching and releasing.

Recovering, Keelen gathered Rowan up in his arms and kissed her deeply.

"You, my love, are an aphrodisiac with a ravenous appetite."

Rowan stood before him naked, her long hair covering her breast. She was about to ask him to join her on the bed when Lady Una opened the door.

"Oh! I see the two of you are still chasing each other around like wild imps."

Lady Una walked over and covered Rowan with a blanket.

"Keelen says I have a large appetite."

"That's why gods and goddesses make the heavens roar."

Tossing his clothes into his lap. "Vardon cancelled tonight's festivities until tomorrow. I suggest you dress and find Amias."

"You are going to miss ordering me around when we return to the castle."

"Wait...Lady Una isn't going with us?"

Lady Una handed Keelen his boots. "Don't worry my dear, Keelen won't be getting rid of me any time soon. Especially when a bairn is born. Now let's get you cleaned up and fed."

Lady Una joined Rowan as she took her meal out in the garden.

"Lady Una, how am I to help our people procreate? One can't possibly think I should be intimate with them all."

Lady Una laughed, "Well that certainly would be an exhausting plight...but no, you won't have to go to that extreme. I, with the aid of the high priestesses, will help you use the power in your well without having to have them drink."

"That's good to hear. Even my appetite isn't that large. Although...my appetite for this food is."

Rowan tore off another piece of bread, lathering it with butter and honey.

Lady Una stood up and wrapped a shawl around Rowan. "Eat up my dear that appetite of yours is only going to get larger."

"What does that mean?"

"I have to tend to some things. I'll be back in a bit."

Lady Una began to hum a melody as she gathered the empty plates before taking her leave.

Rowen found the garden peaceful with the fragrance of wisteria and the warm breeze on her face. It was easy to get lost in her thoughts of Keelen and their future but it wasn't easy to dismiss the overall sensation of being watched.

Rowan knew in an instant that Amias was near, watching her. Instead of fleeing inside the safety of the sanctuary she decided to take matters into her own hands. She remained seated and waited for him to approach her.

Amias had to tread lightly. He wasn't sure how much Keelen had told her of his past or if she suspected his intent. Stepping out from behind an Oak tree Amias took the seat next to Rowan.

Acting as though she was surprised he was there, Rowan began to weave her web.

"Amias! Where have you been?" I have looked all over for you."

"You have?"

"Yes. I have been thinking about what you said...about going to see my mother. And I thought maybe instead of just seeing her we could bring her here."

Rowan looked directly at him when she spoke making sure to rest her hand upon his.

Amias's heart grew hopeful. Maybe his plan was going to work after all. He wanted to reach out and pull her in, to kiss her fully on the mouth, to search for her tongue with his, like he had before Keelen came and stole her.

"I don't think that is wise. Going against Keelens orders." He needed to feel her out a little longer before he set his intent into action.

"You should know by now I don't take orders from anyone...plus, this could be our little secret. No one has to know and we could be back before anyone even notices."

Rowan slipped on her leather sandals. "You'll have to take the lead. I have no idea where the exit is."

"Yes, of course."

Rowan could see the excitement on his face. Slipping her arm through his, she prayed the Gods were with her.

~ like the lighthouse that guides and shines forth its comfort...

Through torrents and turbulence,

It steady and rights one direction

For seeing it knows

It's within reach and reason ~

~ Chapter 9 ~

Nearing the forest Rowan could hear the awakening of crickets and the hooting of owls as they welcomed the setting of the sun. The earthy aroma of damp moss and rotting wood filled the air. With every step Rowan took across the needle-covered path, life began, leaving a trail of forget-me-nots.

Amias's pace was quick and Rowan found it hard to keep up.

"Do you happen to have a knife?"

"Yes, but why? Are you planning on hunting our dinner?" Amias bent down and pulled out a hunting knife. Handing it to her, "Do you know how to use this?"

Rowan rolled her eyes, took the blade and started cutting through the fabric of her dress. When she had finished, a puddle of blue layed on the forest floor and she was sporting a mini.

Amias walked over to retrieve the blade with his eyes fixated on her bare thighs.

"You look like a warrior...a really attractive warrior."

His prowess made Rowan feel uneasy but at the same time alluring, causing her hunger to stir. She had to keep reminding herself that his darkness was too deep, that she wouldn't be able to heal his demons and what she had planned... Had to continue.

Amias's face was so close to hers it felt as though they were dancing without touching.

"You can't possibly be thinking of me as much as I do you," he whispered, running his tongue across her lips, kissed her.

To his surprise Rowan kissed him back. "I've missed you too."

Rowan could hear the high-pitched howl of a fox in the distance.

"We should go before we become a wild animal's meal."

Amias held Rowan's hand as they reached the cliff of rocks. The large boulder that would take her back to the warmth of her mother's arms was covered in climbing moonflowers.

"Amias have you ever thought about not coming back?"

"All the time." Stroking her cheek with the tips of his fingers, "Do you think you can open the veil?"

"I'm not sure but I'm going to give it one hell of a try."

Rowan placed both hands on the boulder, took a deep breath and closed her eyes. She tried to focus on what she had been taught, picturing the rocks density thinning. She thought about the smell of her mother's perfume, the laughter of her friends, and the scent of her lover's skin. She pictured a place of calm and peace, a place that would keep her safe.

What was once hard underneath her hands had opened up, offering a moss covered floor and a chandelier of violet and green crystals. Standing in complete silence, Rowan was in awe.

Yes, she had been here before but there was something different and then she saw it.

Out of the corner of her eye, it was the mural. Rowan tried to look at it without drawing Amias's attention. The mural had changed. No longer stood alone warrior surrounded by the dead, an image of two trees twisted into the others branches had taken its place. Had she opened up the right veil?

Amias wanted one last moment with Rowan before stepping through the other side. He only wished Keelen would be there to witness her last breath. She should have been his, he should be the one to sit on the throne. It all should have been his!

Rowan snapped her fingers. "Hey! Amias...where'd ya go?"

 "Sorry, I was just thinking about the last time we were alone in here."

"Oh? What part?"

Running one hands up her thigh and using the other to draw her in, "How about I just show you."

Amias moved his hand from her thigh to the back of her head, pressed his mouth on hers, parting her lips with his tongue. He liked how short her dress was now, it made it easy for him to get to her. Eager to taste her sweet nectar Amias pushed her against a wall of flowers and with his mouth still on hers he lifted her by her ass, wrapping her legs around his waist.

His excitement for her grew quickly when his fingers swam in the current of her softness and the scent of her musk teased his senses.

Not wanting to raise suspicion Rowan kissed him back. Entwining her hands into his mane, allowing her body to respond to his. She tried to stay focused but as his fingers danced inside her the urge to resist and not surrender to her orgasm was becoming a challenge.

A ledge of rock jutted from the cave wall. Placing her on it, he pushed her dress up and continued to move his fingers in and out. He wanted to drink from her, to quench his thirst but the thought of plunging his hard cock deep inside her grew stronger.

Amias lowered himself between her legs, bending and spreading them wide so he could easily dine. He needed to suckle every last drop out of her. He was determined to make her last feeding memorable.

Her breathing had become heavy as her body willingly opened up to receive the warmth of his mouth and the darting of his tongue. Rowen pushed Amias's head closer and began grinding herself against his mouth. His tongue went deeper and moved with her rhythm, and when he thought he couldn't get enough out of her she trembled and shook.

Still sitting on the ledge and recovering, Rowen watched Amias closely as he stood up and untied his leather wine sack.

"Are you okay? You look a bit flushed."

Swishing the wine around, making sure the belladonna he added was thoroughly dissolved. "It's just warm in here."

Amias went to hand Rowan the wine sack but instead he staggered backward, losing his footing, spilling the poisoned wine on the moss covered floor.

Rowen jumped down from the ledge, straightened her dress and leaning forward,

"Are you sure you're feeling okay?"

Realizing something seriously was wrong, Amias tried to stand but his limbs felt heavy and his head light.

"Something is wrong... please. Go get the healer."

Rowan bent down next to Amias. "Remember those berries you had Nerifina bring to my room? Well... you, my sweet guardian just licked and dined on them. I'm actually surprised you didn't notice its distinct flavor."

Keelen stepped out into the light bringing a smile to Rowan's face.

"Did you have any difficulty finding your way?"

"Not at all. I just followed the bread-crumbs of forget-me-nots. By the way, nice touch."

Keelen, now standing over Amias, "Did you really think I wouldn't be told when you were seen gathering the belladonna? You should thank Rowan for sparing your life dear brother. I really hope you find your peace one day."

Stepping over Amias's slumped body Keelen and Rowan walked out of the cave, closing the veil behind them. Leaving Amias inside to sleep it off.

Walking back to the sanctuary.

"I hope it didn't upset you, watching as …"

Keelen immediately cut her off, "Not at all. You gave him life by saving it. Plus I plan on bedding you as soon as we get back."

Emerging from the darkness of the forest a starlit sky welcomed them. Noticing how Keelen was staring at her, "What? Why are you gawking?"

Keelen laughed, "I'm really liking your new sense of style. You should wear things like that more often."

"I don't think Lady Una would approve."

"Even better."

~ You are a masterpiece of genetic design

With an unlimited capacity for love ~

Her bedroom door opened and closed for the third time. Rolling over and pulling the covers over their heads Rowen kissed Keelens chin.

"How many times are they going to check on us before they realize we aren't leaving this bed?"

"If Lady Una had her way we would already be up."

Keelen placed Rowens hand on his morning hardness. "Speaking of up."

Rowan shook her head. "I'm so sorry my Lord, but no fruit for you until after the ceremony."

The door opened for the fourth time. Keelen uncovered their heads to find Lady Una standing there.

"Well speak of the devil."

Keelen left the warmth of the bed and stood there naked as Lady Una gathered his clothes off the floor.

Handing him the pile, "The item you requested needs your final approval my Lord, so I suggest you dress and stop showing off."

Rowan started giggling uncontrollably watching him follow Lady Una's orders.

Keelen gave Rowan a quick kiss. "You are enjoying this aren't you?"

"Yes I am... My handsome peacock, yes I am."

This time Lady Una joined in on the giggling. Keelen stopped in the doorway, pointing his finger at the two of them. Trying not to take part in the laughter and having to have the last word, "This is so not fair, two against one."

Rowan fell back on the bed smiling.

"Oh that was fun! He has his hands full now!".

Lady Una handed Rowan some clean clothes. "Yes he does. Now let's get you dressed. We have an errand to run."

Rowan slipped into a gown of red and stood in front of the mirror, pinning up her hair. "Are we going far?"

Lady Una stood next to Rowan, took her hand and smiled.

"Not far at all."

Rowan listened while Lady Una recited a few words and like magic, the glass in the mirror changed. No longer could they see their reflection.

Rowan's eyes grew big. "Ho...ly shit! That's my staircase!!"

"Are you going to just stand there with your mouth wide open or are we going to step into the mirror and get your mother?"

Rowan couldn't believe her eyes. There had been a veil there the entire time. Not just in her room but in her house!

"Let me get this straight, the old mirror at the end of my stairs is a veil?"

"Indeed it is. That mirror and this one have been in our family for centuries."

"Our family? I'm so confused."

"Your mother can fill you in."

Rowan's heart was pounding with excitement. She was missing her mom, but didn't realize just how much until she stepped through the mirror. The scent of incense and home-made chicken soup filled the air. She could hear Joni Mitchell playing on the record player, and she immediately knew where to find her mother.

Stepping into the kitchen with Lady Una following behind, Rowan could see her mother at her easel, her long hair pinned up with paint brushes.

"Is there homemade bread to go with that soup?"

Isleen turned around smiling. "What took you two so long?"

After several long overdue hugs, Isleen, Lady Una and Rowan sat at the kitchen table. They spoke of Keelen and the hiccup with Amias and what it was like to meet Vardon over bowls of home-made soup and fresh bread.

"Now that I'm full with your delicious cooking, I think it's a good time to address this list of questions I have stuck in my head. Mom how long have you known about me and why didn't you tell me?"

"I knew what was going to happen long before you were even conceived. The women in our family have a long lineage of being mediums, seers, healers, priestesses, and so much more. Let's just say we have always been close to nature, seen and unseen."

"Well a heads up on what I would be experiencing would have been nice. And Lady Una, how does she fit into all of this?"

"Lady Una is your great-great-great...let's just say there are a lot of "greats" grand-mother."

"This is mind blowing. Does Keelen know all of this?"

Lady Una laddled herself another bowl of soup.

"Rowan, men don't need to know everything."

      After lunch was finished Rowen left her mother and Lady Una to catch up.

Changing into a pair of black leggings with a red mini and a crop-top of Rocky Horror, Rowan felt like herself. She liked the clothes that Lady Una dressed her in but there is nothing like a pair of high-tops and pants. At first Rowan was going to fill a suitcase of her belongings but when her mother informed her that she could go through the veil whenever she wanted, she decided just to grab something special for their wedding night.

Lady Una poked her head through the bedroom door.

"Rowan honey we need to go. We can't be late for the ceremony."

Gathered at the bottom of the stairs Rowan turned to Isleen.

"Mom are you going to be okay seeing Vardon? Honestly, I have no idea what you saw in him...he doesn't talk much."

"Let me handle Vardon and for the record...I like the silent type. They are less likely to say something stupid."

Hand in hand, three strong women stepped through the mirror.

      Rowan's room was buzzing with excitement. Only a few more hours and the entire village would be gathering for the festivities. The union of their Goddess to the young prince, who could now be crowned King. A celebration they had been praying for.

Isleen was taking her time braiding ribbons into Rowan's hair. Telling stories of how she refused to sit still as a child. One would never guess she would bloom into the woman who would calm the earth.

"Who is this raven beauty?" Keelen asked as he walked into the room, his eyes on Isleen.

Lady Una, pushing him back out the door, "That woman is your future mother-in-law, now go...you can't see the bride."

"You've impressed me Lady Una. What other tricks do you have up your sleeve?"

"A lady never tells. What is it you need?"

Keelen handed Lady Una a gift wrapped in linen, "For Rowan."

"I'm sure she will be pleased, my Lord."

Lady Una, shut the door, leaving Keelen standing in the corridor filled with anticipation.

All eyes were on Lady Una when she reappeared

"This, my dear Rowan is your dress."

Rowan stood up from the dressing table.

"I don't understand, I thought I already had a gown?"

"Apparently, Lord Keelen thought you would like this one better. He had it specifically designed for you."

Rowen opened the attached note;

~ My Beloved Rowan,

I've never tried so hard to be alive

As I have for you. You are my pulse.

Adoringly yours,

Keelen ~

Taking her time, Rowan untied the red ribbon. She wanted to treasure every moment of the day. As she lifted the dress up to her chest Rowan was moved by Keelens ability to know exactly what she liked and hurried herself into it.

Lady Una's silence was broken with a, "Where is the rest of the dress?" and an "I'm sure this isn't appropriate attire."

"I think it's perfect," Isleen said as she tightened up the bodice.

Standing in front of the mirror Rowan ran her hand over the white leather mini-dress. The heart shaped neckline was perfect and the train of lace gave it a rocker touch.

Isleen placed a circlet of silver, adorned with moonstone and amethyst crystals upon Rowan's head.

"You have always been my biggest joy and now the world is blessed to call you their goddess. I love you so very, very much."

Rowan hugged her mother tightly, smelling the lavender in her hair.

"I love you more."

"Okay that's enough. You two are going to get all of us blubbering and this is a happy occasion!" said Lady Una, urging them out the door and into the twilight.

****

Rowan couldn't have asked for a more perfect ceremony. Standing barefoot in the middle of the stone circle, she could feel the earth's vibration as hers and Keelen's hands were tied in ribbon. The open field that had been transformed into a magical meadow was the perfect backdrop under a starry sky.

Keelen watched his beautiful wife glow, as she embraced everyone who came to share in their joy. And just when he thought he had exhausted all means of relating his desire and love for her, she always managed to bring more out of him.

Standing on top of a banquet table, Keelen called for everyone's attention.

"I have a special surprise for my beautiful bride. Many of you will not understand what I'm about to do, but she will...and right now that's all that matters."

Keelen stepped down and pulled Rowan into the center of the field, with all eyes on them, he nodded to Isleen.

From a boombox run on batteries, "White Wedding" by Billy Idol filled the air and they danced to "their song."

~ Our love is not a fickle creature

It is a storm

Unrelenting ~

~ Chapter 11 ~

By the light of the moon the newlyweds took their leave with anticipation.

Hand in hand, Rowan walked them to the place where she felt one with the earth. Where the river ran and the air smelled sweet. She smiled to herself knowing soon she'd be making love to the one man who made her feel special. Images of him walking beside her, as they together, heal their land and their people, brought her joy.

"I hope you don't mind my King, I felt this was the perfect place."

"Any place with you is perfect."

Keelen stopped her before she could continue. As much as he enjoyed their conversations, his only desire was to see her naked in the moonlight. Placing his lips upon hers, Keelen kissed her deeply. Pulling away only to look into her green eyes and to whisper how much he wanted her. To him, she was his pulse.

Rowan removed her dress. "Do you like what you see?"

"You my love are a delight to my senses."

Keelen joined his new bride on the soft grass, his fingers tracing the curves of her body.

"And I thought I was the only one with a surprise up their sleeve."

Rowan watched as Keelen slowly unwrapped her.

Moving behind her, he began to unhook her white corset. Leaving light Kisses on her shoulders.

Her hair smelled of roses. Gently kissing her neck, Keelen slid his hand between her thighs finding her lace panties soaked with desire. Running his finger along the edge of lace. "Do you mind if I remove these?"

"Not at all My King."

Keelen skillfully removed the lace between him and her world. A world that was now theirs to share.

Rowan's body felt light and warm. She could feel the hardness of Keelens desire as she moved in circular motions against him. Her heart raced.

Like the veil that had opened and received her, Rowen now opened to Keelen. Allowing him to effortlessly slide within the warmth of her velvet, awakening the dormant screams now echoing throughout the vale.

Juniper

Beyond the Veil